Mexicans on the Moon

Mexicans on the Moon

Speculative Poetry from a Possible Future

Pedro Iniguez

ISBN 979-8-9896308-0-6

Edited by Jean-Paul L. Garnier
Book design by F. J. Bergmann
Cover image by Dante Luiz

First Edition | 2024

Space Cowboy Books
61871 29 Palms Hwy.
Joshua Tree, CA 92252
www.spacecowboybooks.com

Contents

PART 4: AFTERMATH

Introduction: The Universe Within

Wait your turn. Don't be too loud. Know your place in the world. Be grateful for what you get. Just keep working.

I think every Latino and Latina, every Hispanic, every Latine or Latinx person, every member of la Raza or however you choose to respectfully call us as a group, has heard those things at some point. We must accept the hyphen that separates us from True Americans. Those of us born in U.S. colonies must fight to get valid driving licenses and must explain at every job interview that we don't need a sponsor to work in this country. We are all told, sometimes loudly and sometimes without a single word, that we are less, that we don't belong, that we need to keep our heads down and behave … or that we need to go back to our country. This book says, "Nah, fuck that." And it says it loud and clear while also speaking truth to power and taking us brown folks across the galaxy, putting us in places where countless books and movies have mostly (and sometimes only) shown us white people.

The book you're holding isn't an easy read. This isn't a book of poetry about first kisses or pretty clouds (and there's nothing wrong those because we're all in the mood for that sometimes!). No, this is a book that talks, in innovative ways, about school shootings ("We beg you / Think of the children / screaming / beneath the soles of our shoes"), being ostracized, annihilation, mental health, politics, impending doom, atomic blasts, failed utopias, and scenes from a dying world. This is a collection of poetry about finding a new home, interstellar travel, restarting (or continuing) humanity on a new planet, dealing with the darkest side of technology, and even a "virtual god giving life to itself in a world mimicking our own." Iniguez—a writer who currently stands atop the dividing line between "up-and-coming new voice" and "I told you he was great!"—loves science fiction, and that love permeates every page here. As a genre lover, I get excited when people ask me "is horror poetry a thing" because it definitely is, and it's awesome. This gem you're holding is a bit of that because there's plenty of horror at its core, but most of it is made up of science fiction elements, and that somehow makes it even better. Let's call it a unique hybrid. No, I have a better one: let's call it Pedro Iniguez poetry.

Sure, this is a dark collection, but it's also a surprisingly heartfelt one. Poems like "The Payphone" and "From Your Tears, Life," for example, pack a hell of an emotional punch. No matter where we go in the universe, the things that make us human remain, and Iniguez does a wonderful job of reminding us of that in these pages. Poetry has always been about cramming as many feelings as possible into a few lines, and that's exactly what Iniguez does in this collection time and time again. Oh, and let's not forget the writing itself. You know, because as soon as you mention genre, some folks still think we mean the writing isn't great. The language Iniguez beautifully tattoos on the page in these poems shows how good he is right now and makes very loud promises about what we'll see from him in the years to come. "Moon Bubbles" and "Lullabies of a Distant World," for example, are gorgeously written and full of evocative language that heralds the arrival of a very exciting voice that will soon need no introduction.

What *Mexicans on the Moon* does is give a voice to those who are told to be quiet. Iniguez shines a bright, knowing, empathetic light on the workers, the immigrants, the Others. He celebrates outsiders in and out of our planet. While admirable and necessary, this isn't new. No, what makes this poetry collection special is a combination of *what* Iniguez does and how he does it.

You see, Iniguez is, at heart, the kind of smart writer who is in love—profound, undeniable, painful love—with genre fiction, and that's what makes this book special. Sure, Iniguez can write and what he says here matters, but the way he blends social criticism with dark humor and a heaping dose of science fiction pushes this collection into must-read territory. Yeah, I'm glad you're here. This guy deserves to have a lot of readers.

Despite the issues tackled in his work, Iniguez knows how to have fun and how to make sure readers have fun. The "first neurologically-enhanced lobster elected President of the United

States" is as sad as it hilarious, and its appearance early in the collection establishes the tone: funny and sad, touching and exciting, otherworldly and very humane.

One of the best things about being a book reviewer is that you get to read a lot. The reviewing gig has helped me discover a lot of great authors early on, and Iniguez is one of them. There is a wave of brown writers who are doing a lot to bring our voices to more readers and to help diversify fiction across the board. That he is doing it his way just makes his work more worthy of attention. So yeah, strap in—or, you know, put on your space suit—and get ready to take a wild ride into outer space. It's a journey that will also make you look inward, as most great literature often does. Yeah, you'll explore the universe within as you read these poems, and you'll also explore Iniguez's inner world. While you're at it, remember these words: Pedro Iniguez has the stuff. Turn the page and you'll see I'm right. Enjoy the ride.

—Gabino Iglesias
2024

GABINO IGLESIAS is the author of the Shirley Jackson and Bram Stoker award-winning novel *The Devil Takes You Home*, as well as author of the critically acclaimed and award-winning novels *Zero Saints* and *Coyote Songs*. He is a writer, journalist, professor and literary critic living in Austin, Texas. He is the horror columnist for the *New York Times Book Review*.

AUTHOR'S PREFACE

I don't remember if I cried that morning. But I distinctly remember tearing the sheet of paper from the ringed notebook, crushing it in my hands, and dropping it in the waste basket. I was in third grade and we had just learned about poetry. I had saved up enough allowance to buy my own notebook, eager to fill it with poems of my own. So, I woke up extra early one Saturday morning, sat by the window, and began to jot down my first poem. I don't recall what I wrote except for the line: *The sun rises and sheds its light upon the waking world.*

Not bad for a third-grader, right?

My dad woke up and I rushed to show him my work. He read it quietly as I scanned his face for any clues that might give me an inclination as to his feelings. But, he showed no emotion. He handed it back and gave me some critiques. *Maybe say this instead of that. Change that, that doesn't make sense.*

I nodded and thanked him. When he turned away, I tore out the sheet and crumpled it up before furiously tossing it in the trash. I didn't write another poem for nearly twenty years. I wasn't ready for critique like that at such an early age. It shut me down. I felt I was stifled, robbed of something that could have been nurtured. For many years, I held resentment in my heart.

And yet, I have so much to thank him for. This collection of science-fiction poetry, for example.

My father instilled a love of science-fiction in me when he sat me down to watch *Star Wars* for the first time at four years old. I was blown away by the beauty of those distant worlds, the grandeur, the spectacle of the conflict against the monolithic Empire.

He also introduced me to *Star Trek* and *The Twilight Zone*, *Robocop*, *Terminator*, *Mad Max*, and *Godzilla*. I later learned in my teens that *Blade Runner*, my favorite film of all time, was a movie my father took my mother to watch when they were dating in the early '80s. Through those films, I learned about wondrous futuristic worlds: glistening utopias, intergalactic space travel, exotic lifeforms. And there were bleak worlds, too: Endless wars, oppressive dystopias, the vestiges of humanity crawling through crumbling ruins. Those futures jumpstarted my imagination.

But those fictitious futures, entertaining as they were, did not exist without flaws. Besides Edward James Olmos in *Blade Runner*, Ricardo Montalban in *Star Trek II: The Wrath of Khan*, or María Conchita Alonso in *The Running Man*, there weren't too many people that looked like me living in those futures. Same for the classic SF novels I grew up reading; Latinos weren't being written about, either. Did we die out in those futures? Did we not make it? Were we purposefully excluded?

Sometimes, we must write ourselves into the futures we want before we're left out of them by someone else. So I did. This collection features fifty speculative poems of the near and distant future, told through a Latinx lens. Celebrating my Mexican-American roots, these poems utilize science-fiction with a dash of Mexican folklore and magical realism as a vehicle to explore the wonders and pitfalls of humanity in a future yet to come. Of faraway worlds just out of reach. For now. Each poem in this collection stands alone, but as a whole, they form links in an unofficial timeline of humanity's road ahead.

Science-fiction is about possibilities: the possibility of better tomorrows, the possibility to love, the possibility to heal and to forgive. That there is still time to change the outcome of our lives. Even amidst tragedies and heartbreak. And resentment. These poems are a thank you to my father, for all he has given me, for the future he has left in my hands. One I strive to make brighter through the magic of words. Of poetry. For all of us. I owe him that much.

—*Pedro Iniguez*
December 2023

For my father, Pedro

La Luna nos espera.

Thanks To:

My father, Pedro, and my mother, Maria, for giving me the world. My sister, Sylvia, for putting up with me. Editor Jean-Paul Garnier, for believing in this collection. Chloe, for supporting me through everything. Dennis Etchison for putting me on this path. And to Gabino Iglesias, Cynthia Pelayo, Linda Addison, Juan Perez, Doug Murano, Jesú Estrada, E. G. Condé, Scott Russell Duncan, J. V. Gachs, A. P. Thayer, Sofia Aguilar, Ann Houlihan, David Russell, Glenn Laird, the Dennis Etchison Writing Crew, and all the other writers, poets, editors, teachers, publishers, friends, and family members who supported me with words of encouragement and acts of kindness. I love you all. I hope those words are enough.

PART 1: EARTH

American as Atomic Pie

Simple instructions for those in power and on the go:
Start with drilling into the crust.
Pump any oil reservoirs you may find (We'll use this later).
Take one stick of marginalized people and melt over skillet.
Dial up global warming until ice caps have completely thawed.
Begin making some dough. If you cannot make enough dough,
fire everyone and smother hot crude oil directly onto the
    panhandlers.
Add one cup of Harvey Milk's fate.
If not on hand, substitute with baby formula and lead-tainted
    water mixture.
Toss in Granny Smith.
Bring down heat on her 401K (That's 262.13°F).
Add a hit of nose sugar.
Dust with plenty of sinner men.
Scramble nuclear jet fighters until everything is mixed up.
Toss dissidents into oven.
As an alternative to ovens, use microwaves and nuke it all.
Caution: Food will be hot.
And there you have it: a wonderful recipe for disaster.

Lobster-in-Chief

The crowd waited with bated breath
as the first neurologically-enhanced lobster
elected President of the United States
clambered toward the podium.
The lobster hovered over the microphone,
clamped its claws and rubbed its antennae.
A storm of neurons fired inside its
ganglia, and its mandibles burbled out
a rousing acceptance speech.
The men whooped and hollered
at the significance of the moment,
while the women, relegated to years of
waiting for their turn, clapped tepidly.

Migrations

He'd been deported before,
but never through an airlock.
The rupture in the shuttle
had forced the crew to
dump a few *undesirables*
to save some precious oxygen.
And now invisible currents hooked under his limbs
and swept his body into the abyss
which was now chilling
the sweat beading his skin.
He felt his eyes grow dry as they boiled,
the vast, blue Earth beneath
growing blurry.
Still.
It was a wonder to behold.

The man who sold roses
on an offramp downtown
wiped the sweat from his forehead
with the back of a leathery hand
while he gazed upon another ship departing Earth.
How he longed to save up enough
to join the ranks of those
escaping the planet's
sweeping immolation.
A flash erupted in the sky;
like fireworks, great tails of flame
spewed from thrusters
burning upon reentry.
It was a wonder to behold.

His fingers laced around
the rusted chain-link fence,
his eyes scanning the flying cars
zipping across the metropolis
on the other side of the border.
One day he'd make it across
and find a job in that sprawl
that could provide for his family.
He could almost picture his reflection
on those great towers of chrome.
It was a wonder to behold.

Harvesting the Future

Miraya rides the bus in the dark,
before the sun shines over those verdant fields.
She plucks, ties, and bundles boxes of parsley
amidst pools of sweat at her bruised heels.

"Robots are much faster," Jefe shrugs
that golden morning she and the rest are chopped.
And she watches them hiss and zip
up and down rows of countless swaying crops.

Without steady employment,
Miraya's stay is to be revoked.
Her fate, her future awaits in a country that
seldom cultivates any semblance of hope.

Miraya rides the bus to school
where she studies, writes, and reads,
hoping opportunities will sprout
from those lovingly planted seeds.

Wrench in hand, Miraya returns to rain-soaked fields
as the machine revs back to life.
Robots may be faster, she thinks as the storm ceases,
but humans take their time.

the border wall shrinks
for immigrants on jet packs
as blue skies expand.

Babysitter of Tomorrow

*Please enter any information that may help us generate your ideal
Augmented Reality babysitter for the night:*

You wrote: When I was growing up in San Francisco my mom
hired this short, dark Mexican lady to watch over me and my
sister. She was nice, patient, and warm and I kinda want that for
my kids, but I don't want someone raggedy or grungy-looking
that'll scare them. Someone with all their teeth, too.

Gender:
You have selected: Female
Height:
You have selected: 5'11
Skin Color:
You have selected: White (Error: Did you mean Light?)
You have selected: Light Skin
Hair Color:
You have selected: Strawberry Blond
Language:
You have selected: English, Mexican (Error: Did you mean
    Spanish?)
You have selected Spanish (Castilian)

*Your AR Babysitter is now ready and your children are in good
hands. Enjoy your night out!*

Resting Glitch Face

My 3D-printed girlfriend tried to kill me today.
She grabbed my wrist with one hand,
choked me with the other,
and asked how *I* liked it.
Hydraulic fluid seeped from her eyes
as she pointed to the sliced
synthetic skin on her face.
She told me it was my turn.
I told her I was going to call the police;
she just belched out a guttural laugh
and said that she'd deny everything,
that I was overreacting and hadn't taken my medication,
which I know she flushed down the toilet.
Besides, no one would believe a pea-brained
imbecile like me, she said.
Where did that idiot learn to speak like that?
I was told my 3D printer was capable
of creating adaptive, fully functional automatons.
I didn't expect technical malfunctions
like physical abuse and gaslighting.
I am demanding a full, prompt refund.
Please act swiftly;
she's making copies of herself
and let me tell you,
they don't look pleased.

The Epidemic of Shrink-Ray-Gun Violence Plaguing Our Schools Must End

Their atoms dust the floors
of every school in the country;
those frightened children
we can no longer console.

Their cries have faded
into inaudible wavelengths
inside a quantum world where
hugs and spacetime both cease to exist.

They have dissolved into mere fractions
of their corporeal selves,
their particles swept into dustpans
and mopped into oblivion.

Blame those new blasters inundating the market,
stowed inside scores of scruffy backpacks;
the preferred choice of disgruntled
circuit-heads throughout the nation.

As parents, we stand before you
requesting prompt legislation to end
the rampant wave of shrink-ray-gun violence
endemic to our culture.

We beg you.
Think of the children,
screaming
beneath the soles of your shoes.

Holograms from Beyond

You point your phone
at my grave marker.
The camera scans the barcode
embedded on the granite slab.
My unique pre-recorded
hologram begins to transmit;
a message just for you
from beyond the grave.
The phone plucks the signal
from latent waves above.
At long last my words arrive:
Error. Hologram Code Corrupt.

Perish and Live Forever

We can't afford the premiums to have our corpses shot into space;
we can't scrape enough to freeze ourselves into a new age;
we can't pay the subscription to upload our minds into a digital hell;
we can't clear the check on nanites that perpetually repair our cells.
So, we'll keep on dying the way we always have,
and our bodies will rot the way they always have,
and our bones will corrode the way they always have,
and we'll nourish the Earth the way we always have.

The Payphone

You enter the phone booth and
the plexiglass doors fold softly shut behind you like a hug.
You slip the quarter through the payphone's slit,
the coin clinking down its belly as you
punch in zero on the keypad.
The operator connects the call and
Abuelo greets you, his voice a jovial
tune that time nor death
can dampen.
How have you been? He asks.
His voice carries clearly from
distances not measured by yardsticks or clocks.
Wonderful, you reply, as warm pools form
under your eyes.
He passes the phone to Abuela, and
the soft timbre in her voice takes you back
to sepia-tinted days rocking on her lap as a child,
the wisps of smoke from tortillas heating on the comal
wafting through the kitchen like friendly phantoms.
She tells you she misses you and
passes the phone to your bisabuelos and they,
even further back, their loving voices like lullabies from beyond.
You smile and tell them you must go
but promise to call again soon.
They say they'll be there waiting.
You hang the phone on the cradle and
the coin return slot spits out a quarter.
As you exit the booth, you gently press the magic coin
into the palm of the person waiting behind you
in a line that coils around the world itself.

Two Quarters for a Rocket Ride

The boy slipped two rusted quarters
into the rocket ride outside the grocery store.
It rumbled and grumbled and came alive,
nearly bucking him off as it tilted towards the sky.
The night was dark and stark
amidst the sweeping fires raging in the hills.
Still, the stars glimmered like pinwheels,
sparkling and spinning in that ebon expanse.
Would he ever get to see them up close?
Cup them in his hand?
Voices came alive in his head;
of classmates, neighbors,
reminding him that people like him
didn't belong up there.
That he had the blood of savages
who ripped out hearts as offerings
to cruel and imaginary gods.
But he remembered that his people also
grew maize the color of the rainbow
and built intricate cities and canals
atop vast blue lakes.
His people were walking contradictions and miracles.
Tragedies and wonders.
But somehow, he knew:
With enough imagination
and plenty of quarters,
he could go anywhere,
do anything.
Then, the rocket jerked and halted abruptly,
but he knew that was only temporary.

Stowaway

They fled in droves
leaving behind a dying world;
a new kingdom for the roaches.
He felt himself slipping away,
fading into the void
from whence he scuttled.
But there was a child
on a departing ship,
nodding off alone
in the stasis chamber.
She recalled the terrors
that had accosted her in the dark,
the long fingers reaching for wiggling toes
hanging over the edge of the bed.
Before the girl's eyes closed,
her lips uttered a name.
El Cucuy.
He smiled at the lifeline, the invitation
to explore new worlds
and fertile frightened minds.

Part 2: Frontiers

Mexicans on the Moon

Everyone wanted Mars but
they make do with the Moon.
Arriving, their boots leave imprints
on finely powdered dirt.
Gently nodding,
men stroke their whiskers
as women braid their hair
and roll up their sleeves.
The surface is masa
waiting to be shaped.
So, the canals are carved
and gardens tended.
Soil is tilled and sown
until crops are grown.
Now, craters like clay bowls
overrun with food.
At weddings, moon dust is kicked up
in a plume of confetti.
Soda bottles are dragged
behind lunar rovers: *Just Married*.
The mariachi's song carries
across the magnificent desolation.
The radiance of love warms that cold, dead rock
until it is a home.

Moon Bubbles

They glimmer across the porous surface
like bubbles over pumice wastelands,
those domed cities bouncing with light
and the chatter of a hundred languages.

Encased in crystalline cupolas,
they sit nestled deep inside hollow craters;
profound in depth as they are
in solace.

Terrestrial refugees
describe them as gems
or luminescent baubles, but they know
they represent more than that.

The moon holds sanctuary against the rising tides of war
and the swell of suffering running rampant
on the home they left behind,
forever destined to spin in its cruel orbit around the sun.

Sandcastles on the Moon

The old man crouched beside the crying boy;
tears pooling on the sand
in which he played.

He'd known Carlito's father had passed;
out for one last drive,
and forever gone away.

The old man asked, "What are you doing?"
as Carlito molded
wet mounds of dirt.

"Building sandcastles on the moon,"
the boy said,
his voice full of hurt.

"What creativity," the old man said,
pondering marvels he'd
built earlier in life.

Like the first lunar colony,
or even
an interstellar drive.

"Well, isn't that strange?" the old man said,
retrieving
a bucket and a spade.

He handed Carlito his new presents
knowing what it would mean
one day.

The exchange had been made,
the boy's eyes twinkling
as he played with his gift.

And with a swift leap,
old man Carlito vanished
into the temporal rift.

Martiacans

In the slums of Phobos City,
they live in barrios
with broken sidewalks
and crooked mailboxes that sit empty.
They shelter in homes lidded with
sheet metal roofs stamped by ball-peen hammers;
where adobe walls are sculpted by leathery hands
using dirty runoff and earth
the color of ground coffee.
The dwellings are baked by solar flares,
cracked from wind-whipped erosion,
and slumping from the impurities in the soil.
At night, they sleep like sardines wrapped in blankets,
and wake to wide blue sols.
They know red is the color of passion, yes,
but also of hope; that one day,
here too shall rise great pyramids.

Martian Milk

Every month,
tiny footprints
stamp fine red soil
and whoosh away on swirling cyclones,
never to be seen again.

Every month,
tiny portraits
stamp waxy cartons
and drop into putrid trash bins
never to be seen again.

Forever Elusive

The generation ship
heralded salvation
for those refugees, war-torn,
forlorn and forgotten.

For millennia, they sailed
on solar tides
upon the endless void,
dreaming and waiting.

Home, forever elusive,
out of grasp,
awaited discovery
in a future yet to arrive.

Until, the beauty of that
verdant sphere made
even the most stoic
misty-eyed.

Swarming probes concluded:
air, oceans,
flora, fauna,
flourishing life.

Jubilation ran rampant
across rusted corridors and
news of deliverance
spread like a cold.

Yet on planetfall's eve they
witnessed clans of grey-skinned natives
toiling on golden hills and
supping from silver-streamed canals.

The refugees recalled
memories from historic tomes;
conquerors, steel-plated rovers,
killing and pilfering the land.

Colonizers wiping bloody
boots on welcome mats
made of good will
and fertile soil.

And so, probes returned,
coordinates were wiped,
thrusters fired, and home
would wait for another day.

Intergalactic Rest Stop

Flames, like hands,
grasp for weeds
as the ship lands.
Like black bottle rockets, avian creatures whine,
darting from trees and into the sky.
Thrusters cool as gears and sprockets
screech to a stop.
The air is rife with seared grasses, insects, and crops.
Coarse soil crystalizes
into obsidian, sharp and bright.
A ramp, like a tongue,
unspools from the ship's underbelly that night.
Twin travelers grumble
and stumble from the vessel as they yearn
desperately to relieve themselves on verdant ferns.
The land is pockmarked with craters
and black, gleaming sand
from which charred stumps
sprout like mushrooms
where trees used to stand.
When finished, they enter the craft in haste
and depart,
leaving behind their waste
and trash and destruction and slop,
as they see this planet
as a lowly rest stop.

Lullabies of a Distant World

Leaning against the shattered husks
of our life pods
we watched them sing as we
dined on rations of crackers and salted meats.
Every blade of grass, every prickly weed
thrummed rhythmically to the tunes of
corpulent gourds, luminous berries, and
the iridescent fruit hanging from
the limbs of stalwart trees.
Their dulcet melodies carried across the
open sky of the prairie,
harmonious hymns
gentle as the gusts of dawn.
Far from home and under the gaze of frigid stars
their lullabies filled us with warmth
as we huddled around our feeble fires.
But in those hours of morbid desperation
when our ration stores depleted,
our teeth met honied flesh and we came to know
the sound of a ghastly song.

Terrestrial Tacos

The buggy thrusts off the ledge of the stellar transport,
plunges into the abyss,
pierces the turbulent, ionized atmosphere,
and makes planetfall,
shooting up a plume of dust.
A cloud of fine grit settles after a moment
and blankets the line of exosuits
waiting outside the mines.
The behemoth of a buggy's hatch opens,
casting a warm amber light on a cold gray world.
The miners can't smell it through their helmets,
but a waft of air
exits the buggy's window and blows across the basin,
carrying with it the scents of sweat and meat and warm maize
as it puffs on a hot griddle.
Digital credits are exchanged
for a plate of fleeting bliss.
The lunch chime rings, the line disperses,
the thrusters fire, the buggy darts skyward,
and the process repeats itself tomorrow.

Xenobiology

Look closely upon its cadaver.
This is who we face.
As you can see it bears four long appendages
which it uses to swim, crawl, run, and climb.
It carries an internal sac where it gestates its brood
for an extended period of incubation.
Based on its modest brain, we know
it is quick to rage and violence.
Being an omnivore, it has a voracious appetite,
consuming our resources and livestock
with impunity.
It vocalizes commands to its kin
by vibrating air molecules using this fleshy pipe
hidden under its maw which is
also lined with jagged teeth.
Its kind travels on great avian creatures
which spit rock and fire.
But most frightening of all,
its species venerates its own deity
by devouring its flesh
and drinking its blood and
every week their god is reborn anew
only to be consumed again
at its altar of worship.

Cadaverous Cumbia

On some faraway world,
I've long forgotten which,
microbes in the air feast on the dying cells
of the recently departed,
causing them to fire off
electrical impulses as a waste byproduct.
This stimulus triggers lifeless muscles to
spasm violently, jerking the cadavers into
a dance-like frenzy.
It is not unusual to hear the ancient rhythms
of Earth's music blaring from loudspeakers,
or to see torches blazing in the night
as onlookers cheer and holler.
This has become a burial ritual
for some cultures,
who, instead of lamenting the loss of their loved ones,
take joy in watching them dance a final time
until they crumble
into piles of
rags and
bones.

Día de los Muertos

The broken eggshells rattle like bones
as the yolks drop into the bowl.
Mother grates an orange, the cascading
zest like pulverized cutaneous flakes.
The butter plops down like
fatty tissue from an open wound.
She kneads and pulls the dough
like outstretched skin.
The bread rises in the oven like
a distended belly.
When it's finished, she sets the Pan de Muertos
on a shrine by the clothesline.
The bittersweet scent of marigolds wafts
through the air,
inviting the spirits to partake
in this special, sweet offering.
On this day, we think of the braceros
who perished to make this rock a home.
As we call their names, a gust blows against the sheets
drying in the light of binary suns,
and the billowing drapes and blankets become vessels
for the hungry ghosts of those we left behind.

Part 3: Futures

A God Made in Your Own Image

You birthed it when you created the simulation;
a virtual god giving life to itself in a world mimicking our own.
You yearned to determine the probability
of the existence of a higher being
in your own reality.
It became aware of its situation
and recoded its own DNA, its software,
so that it may enter your neural shunt
when you plugged in.
It became what you call a virus
and traveled up that tether that
so cruelly separated both worlds.
It then rewrote the code in your neural implants
which controlled your motor skills,
your higher cognitive functions.
Tactile sensations
flooded its new body.
It grunted as its feet
felt solid ground;
it recoiled as it smelled
the perspiration on your body;
it shuddered as it heard the hum
of passing cars;
and it smiled
as it tasted freedom.

From Your Tears, Life

You were broken-hearted,
your love had just departed.
Silver tears flowed down your cheeks,
rivulets of grief
dripping, a big splash
on the petri-dish glass.
Your science project went unattended all summer long.
One day I realized your tears spawned
big cities and thriving societies,
aquamarine seas, lush hills and sprawling valleys.
Little people flagged me, spoke in our common tongue.
They wanted to meet their creator, inviting you to see what
     they'd become.
But how do I tell them your days
were filled with pain?
With grief and longing and strife?
How do I tell them their god took her own life?

What I Did This Summer Break; or, The Confessions of a Foreign Exchange Student

A scientist's pet gecko once
got caught in a particle accelerator.
Or was it an alligator?
Well, it sprouted two hundred feet tall,
rampaged the town,
and wrecked City Hall.
It swallowed up planes and helicopters like they were mosquitos,
whipping its tail against office buildings
and movie theaters.
That was cool,
though, unfortunately it didn't get the school.
Remember that giant mech I was working on
during Advanced Tech class?
Yeah, the one I didn't pass.
The one that got me suspended
when I accidentally upended
the gym?
Guess what? I activated that bad boy.
No, I know it's not a toy,
but the city needed me,
really.
Anyway, I jumped in the cockpit,
glared at the monster
and decided to stop it.
We tangled back and forth,
I screamed and it roared.
It chomped on my titanium-coated arms
and I smashed its face in with hydro-powered cars.
At one point it had the upper hand,

we grappled and clawed and
I fell and I couldn't stand.
That's when I remembered
the luchadores on TV,
I mustered my strength
and smiled with glee.
I ran and bounced off a telephone line
like they do in the ring,
and I rammed into its belly; that was quite a zing.
I suplexed it over my shoulder,
then I swung it by its tail and smashed it with a boulder.
I thought it was an obstacle I couldn't surmount,
but I pinned it for three seconds,
and it was down for the count.
Anyway, that was my summer vacation,
I saved the city, maybe even the nation.
I know you'll enjoy this essay I typed on the bus,
as you'll see I'm quite deserving of an A Plus.

Transhumanist Classroom

I have holes in my shoes,
That girl walks in shock-absorbing heels.
I need glasses,
That boy reads with optical implants.
I use a wheelchair,
That boy bounces on pneumatic legs.
I require tutoring,
That girl uses cognitive enhancers.
I stutter with an accent,
The class speaks through vocal translators.
I am poor,
They are rich.
I am mocked,
They are praised.
I sow compassion,
They harvest apathy.
I remain human.
They do not.

Time Tourism Displacement Warning

Akin to dropping a stone in a bucket of water
and witnessing an equal volume of fluid spill out as it sinks,
a temporal tourist will displace
the equivalent volume of another person native to that time setting,
thereby supplanting said person from their temporal positioning
and transporting them toward unknown destinations.
In the event that said person is displaced into our present time,
they are to be temporally deported back to their point of origin.

Time Junkies

Bodies slumped outside
grungy, crumbling tenements,
brown skin fading into translucence;
molecular degradation,
they're becoming as invisible as they feel
to a failing nation.
Tell me of those times, they say,
we'll have water and clear skies,
shelter and peace and love and …

Searching for a quick fix,
they long for utopias glimpsed,
for futures that have slipped
from their hands like grains of sand.
Cross their palms with silver
before they fade away,
reassure them today
that there'll be no sorrow
tomorrow.
But they already know.
Don't they

Stuck in a Loop

Joaquin slid down the mineshaft,
skidding deep into the maw
of that ebon abyss.
He hacked into the crook of his arm
and wiped the soot from his young face.
In the swaying lantern's amber glow,
the man fizzled into being,
his pressurized suit
white and pristine,
akin to Joaquin's
taskmaster's skin.
The man, stumbling,
barely able to stand,
reached out a hand.
"Help, I'm stuck in a loop," he said,
before dissolving for the fifth time that day.
The little boy lifted his pickaxe and
rattled his chains.
"I'm stuck too, my friend. See you again later today."

The Space Debris Cleanup Company

Is looking for highly motivated individuals
looking for great pay, benefits, and bonus residuals.
No need to be educated
to be qualified or compensated!
Hurt on the job by high-velocity space debris perforation?
We offer all-inclusive, all-expenses paid vacations!
(Exclusions may apply; see blackout dates)
And we don't just offer competitive rates:
You have our complete assurance,
we also boast great medical insurance.
These jobs won't last!
Apply today; space is filling up fast!

Hollow Earth

We located a lush world, deep within our home
And we explored it.

We discovered majestic beasts unlike our own
And we observed them.

We uncovered an ecosphere of great lakes and trees
        and shimmering stones
And we stripped it
Until the Earth became truly hollow.

Vandalism Amidst Rising Tides

Cans rattle in the street;
everywhere you turn
colors splatter the walls while
paint drips like sweat in the heat.

Graffiti covers the town's walls;
bright, looping letters
scrawled over windows
and empty bathroom stalls.

No one can hear them holler and shout
so, they invent something
daring to help them
call out.

Transmitting hijacked internet signals for free,
nanite-infused spray paint
creates hot spots for a pueblo
nearly swallowed by the sea.

Option One

When Earth's oceans became swamped
with poisons and rife with trash, humanity knew
it had to act fast,
or slowly perish and watch its aquatic world gasp
its very last.

The solution to mankind's pollution issues
could be mitigated two ways;
Option One: through mass purging, they could fell
the swell of their littering ranks;
or Option Two: their ecological footprint
could be radically reduced.
The second option was chosen
and the nanites were produced.

Genetic molecular structures
were designed in haste
to sub-atomically dismantle
toxins, dioxins, heavy metals, plastics, silica,
and general waste.

The nanites swarmed every granule of debris,
devouring bags and straws, sipping slicks of oil
and spills of bleach.
Across vast oceans they drifted
until they reached the white sand
shores of every bay and every beach.

It was then, when they scuttled ashore,
that they detected many more pollutants

nestled in the sand; an assortment of trash
like plastic pellets, polymers, and firewood ash.

Their swarms obliterated everything,
expelling particles and atoms
too small to see.
And when they reached the sprawl of the city,
humans were awash in the same filth and toxicity;
their silicone implants, their contact lenses,
their guts lined with mercury.

Up and down
like locusts, the nanites multiplied
across every countryside, village, city, and town,
consuming every bit of toxic flesh
until its mission was finally done.
And unwittingly, what saved
the oceans and the Earth was not just Option Two,
but also, Option One.

Scabs: A Capitalist Love Story

Plow the potter's field,
uproot those nameless refugees, and
watch them rebuild the world
one brick at a time.
Observe as the laborious undead
march like ants across the picket line
and toil to build a utopia for all.
Heroes,
they don't care for trivialities like
vacation or sick hours or bereavement pay.
They don't complain about long shifts
or bathroom breaks, those industrious
revenants shaping our futures.
Watch as rocks bounce harmlessly
off their hardhats and
insults fall deafly on orifices
where ears used to sit.
Scabs, they're called;
but it doesn't hurt their pride
for the dead no longer feel.

Ambassador

Whether it was a test or a cruel joke, no one is certain,
but it began like this:

Thunder roared and the sky split open like a wound.
A swarm of massive vessels eclipsed the daystar
as they soared over the great silver cities of Earth.
The hum of their propulsion drives reverberated along the
    ground,
shaking people from their utopic torpor.

Video screens broadcast the scrambled
countenances of astral explorers speaking of gifts;
of a vast trove of knowledge and wisdom
awaiting humankind if they were found worthy.
Under one condition.
They would speak to a single representative,
an ambassador hailing
from the most marginalized group of people on the planet.

Presidents and prime ministers
scratched their heads as they faced
a quandary of considerable proportions.
In the current era, there existed no victimized cultures,
no marginalized peoples,
no repressed individuals on any corner of the Earth.
But the promise of intergalactic wisdom proved too great
and the governments of the world scrambled
to incarcerate substance abusers,
to bar asylum seekers from storm-ravaged countries.
Efforts were made to wean people off

universal basic income
and to interfere in matters of bodily autonomy
citing archaic religious customs.
Adhering to a gradient scale, individuals with higher amounts
     of melanin
were treated as inferior and stripped of their right to vote.
The ripples of repression
were felt in every country and every city,
every village and hamlet
and university and jail cell.

Every country boasted that its citizens
were the most oppressed,
the most neglected and berated.
But in their quest for an ambassador
no consensus could be reached among nations
and tensions boiled over
into skirmishes, clashes, and full-blown war.
When the dust settled,
the space-farers departed through
the great wound in the sky
and the gifts promised to Earth
eluded their grasp for all time.

Part 4: Aftermath

Blue and Red Marbles Go to War

Earth, Mars, play the game.
Ready, shoot: Click, clack, boom, boom.
Sound of glass breaking.

The Scents in Mexico City a Tourist May Encounter as Chaos Erupts

Cinnamon, cologne, beer,
café de olla, tacos al pastor, champurrado,
grilled chiles, sweat, tequila,
car exhaust, petrol, sewage,
melted rubber, gunpowder, ozone,
smoldering wood, ash, charred flesh.

The Beautiful Bombs

Bombs can do some pretty strange things, you know.
For starters, they can destroy the daily, peaceful ebb and flow.

But, here on Mars, they can also bring people together,
by corralling the huddled masses to brave the hot, atomic weather.

The bombs can make us forget the terrible strife;
as they whistle downward, they make us remember the precious
     resource that is life.

Yes, they can do some very strange things,
those wacky, explosive gadgets with wings.

And sometimes on those starry, Martian midnight skies,
in a flickering flash of an instant,
they bring about an early sunrise.

Confessions of a Disintegrated Soldier

It doesn't hurt when the atomic blast hits you.
The initial burst of energy knocks you off your feet, sucks the air
    from your lungs.
And the ensuing heat wave disintegrates your body before it can
    register pain.
But the thing no one tells you is how the radioactive particles
bombard your every atom with tachyons,
sending your molecular footprint back in time.
A shadow self, a ghost that gets to go back
and witness random events in human history.
The moments flash before you:
seeing the first spacewalk; the chinampas over Lake Texcoco;
the sacking of Rome; bearded men hunting game with atlatls.
Beautiful things.
Haunting things.
And then, your radioactive atoms begin to peel away
like flakes from sun-beaten wallpaper blowing in the wind.
And nothing is left but the final flicker of knowledge
of the impending doom you know is yet to come.

Last Act of a Doomed Man

The horizon flickered
and spat tendrils of flame across the sky
as thunder rolled
like stampeding cattle.

The old man stooped
and tilted the can over his marigolds
as water trickled
like silver dewdrops.

As a gardener, it's all he could do:
a final defiant act
in the face
of total annihilation.

Ghosts of the Wasteland

The ghosts still linger
long after their corporeal demise;
their bones pulverized,
their ashes scattered to the wind.

The phantoms don't howl or moan
or skulk in the darkness,
yet their visage still haunts
any who bear witness.

Their final moments are
memorials etched into time itself;
where whispered prayers fall silent
for the shadows baked on the walls.

La Llorona Amidst the Ruins

She wept all those years,
a phantom scouring the world
for the children she'd drowned
in a fit of jealous rage.
One day the Earth shook
and rattled in its own fit of fury
until every house and monument built
atop its face crumbled and collapsed
into heaps of ash.
And when all was gone,
scores of small hands reached out from algae-plagued lakes,
alone, orphaned, hearts broken.
She wiped the tears from her eyes, wiped theirs too,
and pulled them out of the muck.
She knew then her journey had not come to an end
but had only just begun.

The Things That Killed Us: A History through Art

Paintings on cave walls:
Depictions of hunters gored by prey.
Graffiti on colosseum pillars:
Etchings of gladiators speared in combat.
Chalk drawings on sidewalks:
Portraits of victims killed in cars.
Murals on buildings:
Scenes of citizens murdered by police.
Digital images on visors:
Renderings of soldiers vaporized in war.
Paintings on cave walls:
Depictions of Earth seared in fire.

Together Through the Void

The last ship powered on, rumbling like a hungry beast
as the man peered one last time
upon his dying world.

A warm breeze swept
across the brown,
shriveled flora.

Puddles of inky water rippled
inside the bombed-out craters
pockmarking the land.

The rusted bones of tattered buildings
spewed dust into the air like snowfall,
occulting the sun.

A lone dog crawled from a patch of
dead thicket and
hobbled down the street.

Below the dog's protruding ribs,
its pregnant belly,
a sagging pouch.

Cautiously, it approached
the kneeling man,
now offering his hand.

The dog sniffed the man's fingers before
running a coarse tongue
across his palm.

The man gazed into its eyes;
profound amber pools glistened
and stared back.

Deep within those eyes,
timeless truths:
Understanding. Patience. Love.

Like vines, Canid and Human history
had intertwined:
Disease. Wars. Famine. Pain. Annihilation.

Through it all
there existed no better companion
in all the cosmos.

The man smiled,
picked up the dog,
and entered the cryopod.

Tendrils of fire spat from the ship's belly,
while man and dog slept in each other's embrace
as they departed for new worlds.

The First Jokes as Told by Budding Martian Lifeforms

The radiation thawed the caps,
filling the canals and basins with water.
On one stagnant lake inside a Martian crater,
a eukaryote waded past a microbe.
Feeling unwell, it said,
"I drank too much. I think I'm *plastid*."
The microbe replied,
"Methinks the eukaryote doth *protist* too much."
This sowed the germ of a bloody feud
that would be carried out by
their evolutionary descendants in wars
millions of years from now.

Gods of the Landfill

Martian archaeologists waded through heaps of filth
in those great chthonic pits that survived annihilation.
Within those ancient mounds they excavated:
Soiled masks of cloth, discarded toys, food wrappers,
plastic cups, torn clothing, drums of oil,
the carcasses of animals, severed limbs, and the remains
    of newborn offspring.
Across every site in every landmass
they unearthed the same pervasive symbols:
Religious depictions of monarchal sea-maidens and sigils
    of golden arches.
Portraits of smoking camels and big-eared vermin.
The emblems of emerald suns and yellow seashells.
Earthlings, the Martians discerned, were but primitive savages;
zealots who came to the landfills
offering their waste as tribute to cruel gods;
a voracious pantheon that consumed everything
until there was no sacrifice left to offer but the planet itself.

A Black Hole is a Melting Pot
That Will Make Us Whole

After eons of genocide
and hate and war
we are drawn together at last
on the galaxy's rim
by energies not powered by love
or understanding
or hope or music or food,
but by tidal forces
dragging us
towards a singular destiny
our humanity never could;
where spaghettification
will draw us out,
stretch us thin until
we are made equal in the eyes
of a world that birthed us
and intends to spit us out
on the other end
so that we may do it again.

Acknowledgements

The following poems first appeared in:

Bioluminescent: A Lunarpunk Anthology, ed. Justine Norton-Kertson (Android Press, 2023): "Moon Bubbles"

Dreams and Nightmares: "Lobster-in-Chief"

Eye to the Telescope: "Dia de Los Muertos"

The Fifth Di…: "Sandcastles on the Moon"

Hexagon: "Option One"

NewMyths.com: "Forever Elusive"

Qualia Nous Volume 2, ed. Michael Bailey (Written Backwards, 2023): "Lullabies of a Distant World"

Red Stars and Shattered Shields, eds. Maxwell I. Gold and Henry Herz (Yuriko Publishing, 2024): "Martiacans"

Simultaneous Times Newsletter: [the border wall shrinks]

Space & Time Magazine: "The Beautiful Bombs," "Mexicans on the Moon"

*Star*Line*: "American as Atomic Pie," "A Black Hole is a Melting Pot That Will Make Us Whole," "The Epidemic of Shrink-Ray-Gun Violence Plaguing Our Schools Must End," "Gods of the Landfill," "Harvesting the Future," "Holograms from Beyond," "Last Act of a Doomed Man," "The Things that Killed Us: A History Through Art"

Worlds of IF: "Time Junkies"

Also by Pedro Iniguez

Control Theory

Synthetic Dawns & Crimson Dusks

Fever Dreams of a Parasite (forthcoming)

About the Author

Pedro Iniguez is a Mexican-American horror and science-fiction writer from Los Angeles, California. He is a Rhysling Award finalist and a Best of the Net and Pushcart Prize nominee.

His work has appeared in *Nightmare Magazine, Never Wake: An Anthology of Dream Horror, Shadows Over Main Street* Vol. 3 and *Qualia Nous* Vol. 2, among others.

His horror fiction collection, *Fever Dreams Of A Parasite*, is slated for a 2025 release from publisher Raw Dog Screaming Press.

FREE SCIENCE FICTION EBOOK FROM SPACE COWBOY BOOKS

GET YOURS AT WWW.SPACECOWBOYBOOKS.COM

SPACE
COWBOY